D0923544

The Great PUMPKIN SMASH

by Lori Haskins Houran
illustrated by Maarten Lenoir

Kane Press
New York

story

For my Florida friends.
I miss you!—L.H.H.

To Mum and Dad, for their
continued support.—M.L.

Library of Congress Cataloging-in-Publication Data

Names: Houran, Lori Haskins, author. | Lenoir, Maarten, illustrator.
Title: The great pumpkin smash / by Lori Haskins Houran ; illustrated by Maarten Lenoir.
Description: New York : Kane Press, 2020. | Series: Makers make it work |
Summary: "When he moves to Florida, Luke misses autumns in Maine and decides to
build and engineer a pumpkin catapult for the local park to help them recycle leftover
jack-o'-lanterns"—Provided by publisher.
Identifiers: LCCN 2019009874 (print) | LCCN 2019020584 (ebook)
| ISBN 9781635922691 (ebook) | ISBN 9781635922684 (pbk) |
ISBN 9781635922677 (reinforced library binding)
Subjects: | CYAC: Catapult—Design and construction—Fiction. | Pumpkins—Fiction. |
Moving, Household—Fiction.
Classification: LCC PZ7.H27645 (ebook) | LCC PZ7.H27645 Gp 2020 (print) |
DDC [E]—dc23
LC record available at https://lccn.loc.gov/2019009874

10 9 8 7 6 5 4 3 2 1

Kane Press

An imprint of Boyds Mills & Kane, a division of Astra Publishing House

www.kanepress.com

Printed in the United States of America

Makers Make It Work is a registered trademark of Astra Publishing House.

Luke looked up at the sky. He sighed.

It was fall. But instead of red and yellow leaves, he saw green palm trees.

Luke had moved from Maine to Florida over the summer. At first it hadn't seemed that weird. Sure, it was hot. Maine got hot, too.

But fall was different. Luke missed cool air and fresh apple cider. Most of all, he missed pumpkin chucking!

"What's pumpkin chucking?" asked Ben. He was Luke's new friend from upstairs.

"You go to a farm and put a pumpkin in this big wooden thing called a catapult," said Luke. "Then you chuck it really far. When it lands, pumpkin guts smash everywhere!"

"Cool!" said Ben.

"Hey, let's build a catapult here!" said Luke.

"Where?" asked Ben. "Dude, we live in an apartment building."

Luke sighed again. Ben was right.

A catapult is a machine used to hurl objects. Ancient Greeks invented the catapult to fling spears at their enemies.

The next day, Luke's mom plopped a bag of candy pumpkins in front of the boys.

"Here," she said. "You can build a mini catapult!"

Luke shrugged. "I guess."

Ben searched for instructions on his phone. A website came up. *Be an engineer! Build your own miniature catapult!*

"This looks easy," he said.

Everything they needed was in the junk drawer. Popsicle sticks. Rubber bands. Glue and a bottle cap.

They put the catapult together in just a few minutes.

"This top stick is the arm," Ben said. "Glue the bottle cap on it, then we're all done."

Engineers design and build things. Toys, phones, cars, bridges—all these things were created by engineers.

"It's ready!" Luke said when the glue was dry. Ben loaded a candy pumpkin into the bottle cap. He pressed the arm down and let go. The candy flew a few feet and bounced on the table.

"It works!" Ben said.

"My turn," said Luke.

Luke pushed down hard on the arm. *Zing!*

His pumpkin sailed over the edge of the table!

"Whoa! Yours went so far!" Ben said.
"Maybe because I pushed down more?"
Luke said.

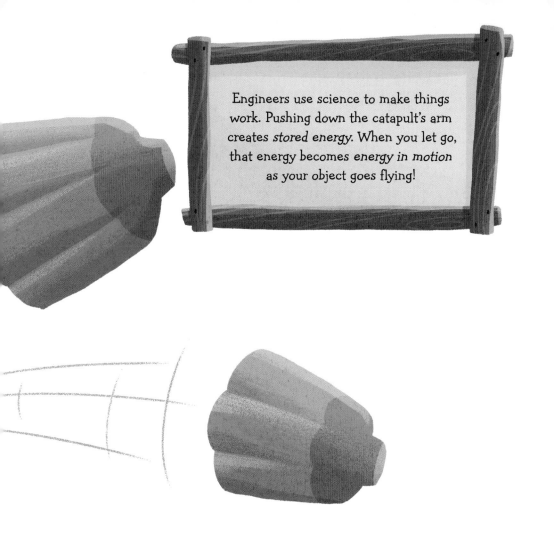

Engineers use science to make things work. Pushing down the catapult's arm creates *stored energy*. When you let go, that energy becomes *energy in motion* as your object goes flying!

They tested it out. Sure enough, the more they pushed the arm down, the farther the candy went. Before long, pumpkins were flying all over the kitchen!

"This rocks!" Ben said. "But I still wish I could try real pumpkin chucking with you."

Luke's grin faded a little. "Me, too."

On Friday, Luke and his mom bought a pumpkin. They got it at the grocery store, not a farm. Weird.

Luke's mom spread out a newspaper to carve on. "Hey, check this out." She pointed to a box on the page.

Don't toss those pumpkins!

Please don't throw your jack-o'-lanterns in the trash. They take up space in our landfills. Instead, drop them off for composting. November 7 at Draper Park.

"Composting was my idea," she said proudly. Luke's mom worked at the park, fixing things. "I just hope people come."

"Is composting where you smash up old vegetables?" Luke asked.

"Yup, to make fertilizer," his mom said.

"Does it matter if the vegetables are already smashed?" asked Luke.

His mom shook her head. "I don't think so."

Luke jumped up. "I know how to get people to compost. Pumpkin chucking! In the park!"

"Oh my gosh!" cried his mom. "What a great idea!"

They drove straight to Draper Park and found Ms. Dane, the parks director.

"That IS a great idea!" she agreed. "But the event is next weekend. We don't have a catapult."

Engineers look for ways to be useful. What can they create that will fill a need in the world?

"I'll build it—with my friend Ben!" said Luke, "We just made one!" He didn't mention that it was made out of Popsicle sticks.

Luke's mom smiled. "I can help them. I'll make sure everything is safe and sturdy."

"Wonderful!" said Ms. Dane. "I'll call the newspaper and spread the word!"

Luke's mom unlocked a toolshed in the park. "Everything we need should be here."

"Can you believe we're building a real pumpkin catapult?" Luke asked Ben when he got there. "Look—instead of Popsicle sticks, we can use these boards."

Ben picked up a bucket. "This is like a big bottle cap," he said.

"And these bungee cords are like huge rubber bands," added Luke. "What else do we need?"

Ben got out his phone for instructions. "Is there a piece of pipe?" he asked.

"Right here!" called Luke's mom.

"First we have to build a frame," said Ben.

He and Luke measured some boards. Luke's mom cut them. The boys screwed them together.

Next Ben asked Luke's mom to drill a hole all the way through another board. Luke slid the pipe into the hole. The ends of the pipe fit into the frame. Now their catapult had an arm.

"This is looking good!" said Luke.

"We should stop for now," his mom said. "You have to get ready for Halloween tonight!"

SAFETY TIP: Never use drills or saws without an adult's help.

Luke and Ben went trick-or-treating right in their own building.

"Isn't it awesome?" said Ben. "We get tons of candy!"

Luke looked in his bag. Yup, he had way more candy than last year. Florida wasn't all bad!

The boys got back to work the next morning. Ben even brought a pumpkin to the park. "To test the catapult," he said.

"Good thinking," said Luke's mom.

Ben checked the instructions again. He showed Luke's mom where to screw bolts onto the frame and arm.

Then the boys hooked the bungee cords to the bolts.

The last step was screwing the bucket onto the arm. Luke and Ben took turns using the screwdriver.

"Okay," said Ben. "Let's try it!"

The catapult was so tall, they needed a ladder to load Ben's pumpkin.

"Get ready for major chunks!" Luke pressed down on the arm and let go.

The pumpkin plopped on the grass a few feet away.

"So much for major chunks," said Ben.

THUD

"What went wrong?" asked Luke.

Ben frowned. "Remember the mini catapult? The more we pushed the arm down, the farther the candy went."

"What if we *pull* the arm down?" Luke said. "Then we can get it all the way to the ground."

They hooked a rope to the arm and pulled down, down, down. Luke put the pumpkin back into the bucket. Ben let the rope go.

Zing! The pumpkin sailed across the park. *BAM!* It hit the ground. It exploded into gooey orange chunks.

"Woo-hoo!" yelled the boys. They high-fived Luke's mom.

The catapult was ready. Luke couldn't wait for composting day!

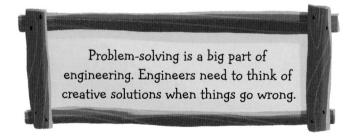

Problem-solving is a big part of engineering. Engineers need to think of creative solutions when things go wrong.

At last, November 7 came. It started off
chilly—not at all like normal Florida weather.
"Brr!" Luke's mom said. "I need a jacket!"
She drove Luke and Ben to Draper Park.
When they got there, it was packed!

Kids ran around with jack-o'-lanterns for
chucking. A ranger handed out cups of cider.
Cool air, hot apple cider, and pumpkin chucking?
"It's like I'm in Maine again!" Luke said happily.

"Ready for the first launch?" Ms. Dane called to Luke and Ben.

"Ready!" said Luke.

Ben set up the catapult. Luke loaded his jack-o'-lantern. They let it fly.

SMASH!

Catapults aren't just for pumpkin chucking! They're also used to launch planes off aircraft carriers.

The whole crowd cheered!

All day, Luke and Ben showed kids how to chuck their pumpkins. Afterward, everyone helped shovel the pumpkin pieces into a truck for composting.

"We got so many pumpkins!" Luke's mom said.

"It was a *smashing* success," Ms. Dane agreed. "Will you two do pumpkin chucking for us next year?"

Ben and Luke looked at each other. "YES!" they whooped.

Luke smiled. Fall in Florida might always be a little weird. But for at least one day a year, it would feel just right.

Learn Like a Maker

Luke missed fall in Maine, especially the pumpkin chucking. But he didn't let Florida's hot weather get in his way. He saw a problem. Then, like any good engineer, he figured out how to fix it!

Look Back

- After reading page 3, find Maine and Florida on a map. What do you know about the two states?
- Reread pages 22–25. What was the problem with the catapult? How did Luke and Ben's earlier engineering experiments help them to solve it?

Try This!

Build a mini catapult

What you'll need: 7 wooden craft sticks, 3 rubber bands, glue, bottle cap, mini marshmallows

1. Stack five craft sticks and wrap rubber bands around both ends to make the base.

2. Stack the other two craft sticks. Wrap a rubber band around one end of this stack to make the arm. Glue the bottle cap to the other end of the arm. Let it dry.

3. Slide the base between the two craft sticks of the arm. Then secure it with a rubber band.

4. Put a mini marshmallow in the bottle cap, push the arm down, let go, and watch your marshmallow fly!

Bonus! Engineers like to experiment. Make the base of your catapult bigger by adding five more Popsicle sticks. How does that change your catapult? Get a tape measure and see how far your marshmallow flies now!